Designed by Flowerpot Press in Franklin, TN.
www.FlowerpotPress.com
Designer: Stephanie Meyers
Editor: Katrine Crow
ROR-0808-0109
ISBN: 978-1-4867-1263-2
Made in China/Fabriqué en Chine

HORSEY, HORSEY

MELISSA EVERETT

ILLUSTRATED BY IVANA FORGO

HORSEY, HORSEY, let's go play.
HURRY UP! It's the perfect day!
An ADVENTURE
just for ME and YOU.
HERE WE GO, it's just us two!

HORSEY, HORSEY, don't you stop.
Let your feet go CLIPPETY CLOP.
Your tail goes SWISH
and your WHEELS go 'round.
GIDDY UP! We're outward bound.

HORSEY, HORSEY, we love to play,
so let's GET GOING, on our way!
Your tail goes SWISH
and your WHEELS go 'round.
GIDDY UP! We're outward bound.

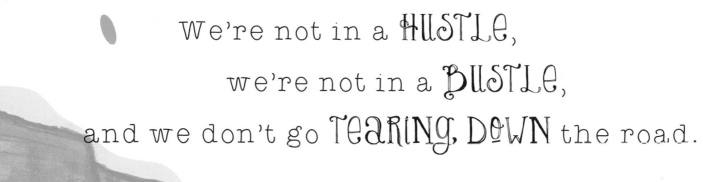

We're not in a HUSTLE,
we're not in a BUSTLE,
and we don't go TEARING, DOWN the road.

We're not in a HURRY,
we're not in a FLURRY,
and we don't have a very HEAVY LOAD.
So...

HORSEY, HORSEY, don't you stop.
Let your feet go CLIPPETY CLOP.
Your tail goes SWISH
and your WHEELS go 'round.
GIDDY UP! We're homeward bound.

HORSEY, HORSEY, no need to run.
The world is full of SO MUCH FUN!
Your tail goes SWISH
and your WHEELS go 'round.
GIDDY UP! We're homeward bound.

We love to EXPLORE
and SEE what's outdoors,
and we both really love to ROAM.

We love to PLAY,
but at the END OF THE DAY,
we both love to end up at HOME!
SO...

HORSEY, HORSEY, don't you stop.
Let your feet go CLIPPETY CLOP.
Your tail goes SWISH
and your WHEELS go 'round.
GIDDY UP! We're homeward bound.